# I love dogs

## Written by Ann Miller
## Illustrated by Steve Pileggi
## Spanish Translation by Sylvia Aguera

Jaylil Publishing Company

Library of Congress Cataloging-in-publication Data

Jaylil Publishing Company
Post Office Box 656551
Flushing, New York 11365

ISBN 0-9748165-2-3

# For Autumn and Thaiann

I love dogs all kinds of dogs.
Amo a todas clases de perros.

Poodles and huskies and collies and rottweilers.

2 Los pulis y los huskies y los collies y los rottweilers.

**Chihuahuas and bull dogs and grey hounds and terriers.**
**los Chihuahuas y los bulldogs y los perros galgos y los terriers.**

3

Dogs are fun, they can do many things.
Los perros son muy divertidos, ellos pueden hacer muchas cosas.

4

Did you know that dogs were man's best friend?
¿Sabías que los perros se conocen como el major amigo del

5

Once I had a dog that was bigger than me.
Una vez tuve un perro que era más grande que yo.

6

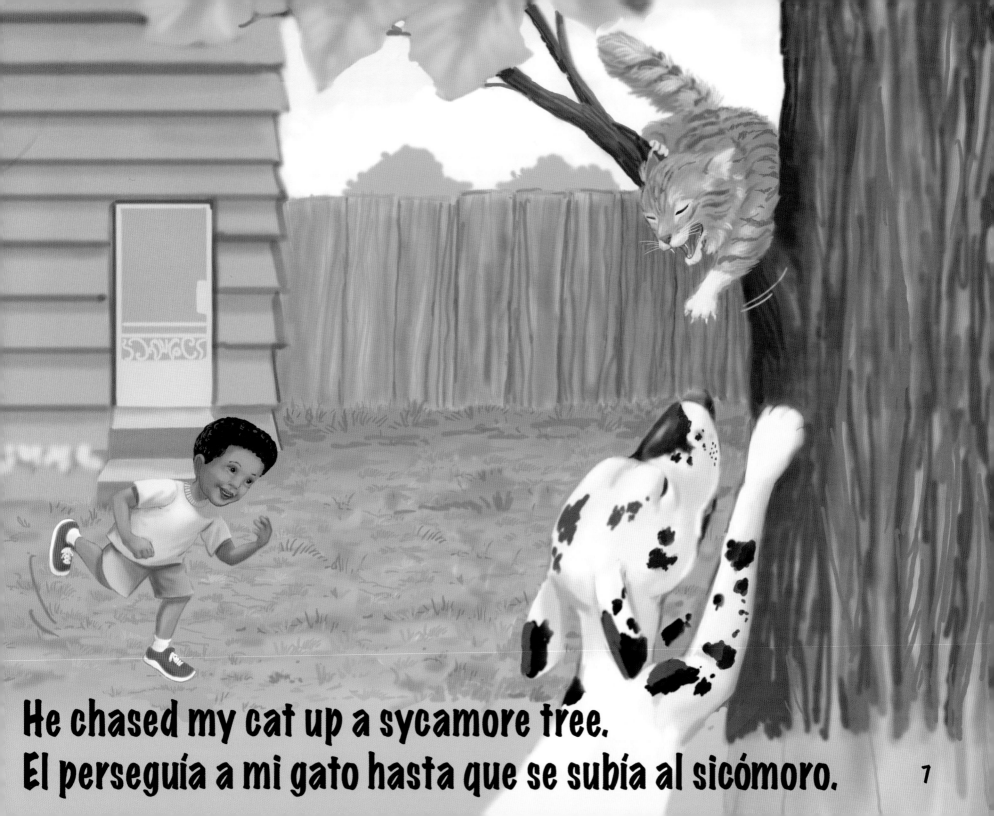

He chased my cat up a sycamore tree.
El perseguía a mi gato hasta que se subía al sicómoro.

7

My dog is happiest when we play outside.
Mi perro está más contento cuando jugamos afuera.

8

Once I took my dog on a pony ride.
Una vez llevé a mi perro a pasear sobre un potro.

Dogs can dive and dogs can swim.
Los perros pueden nadir y tirarse al agua.

The dog-paddle swim style is named after them.
El estelo de nadir como un perro se dice porque así es como lo hacen los perros.

I love dogs all kinds of dogs.
Amo a todos tipos de perros.

12

**Dalmatians and miniatures and dachshunds and welsh corgis.**
**Los dálmatas y los minaturas y los dachshunds y los corgis de gales.**

I entered my dog in the local show.
Inscribí a mi perro en una demostración local de perros.

14

She won the blue ribbon; she was the best by far.
Ella ganó la medalla azul; era la major entre todos.

# Best in Show

DEAR GRAND-MA: WE WON THE BLUE RIBBON.
MY DOG WAS THE BEST IN THE SHOW.
HOPE YOU LIKE
YOUR POST CARD.

LOVE, ASA

**We had our faces on a picture post card.**
**Pusieron nuestras caras en una postal.**

We made copies for our friends, we were so proud.
Hicimos copias para nuestros amigos, estábamos tan orgullosas.

17

My dog is smart, yes she's real cool.
Mi perra es inteligente, sí ella es muy cool.

18

She carried my books, as we walked to school.
Ella me llevaba los libros mientras caminábamos a la escuela.

All of the dogs have colorful coats.  They stand in line as we dress them up.
Tosos los perros tienen abrigos de muchos colores.  Se ponen en fila mientras los vestimos

20

I love dogs all kinds of dogs
Amo a todas clases de perros.

**Greyhounds and Chihuahuas and dachshunds and beagles.**
**Los galgos y los Chihuahuas y los dachshunds y los beagles.**

22

Saint Bernards and welsh corgis and bulldogs and mastiffs.
Los san bernardos y los corgis de gales y los bulldogs y los mastiffs.

**Pekingese and malamutes and Mexican hairless.**
**Los pekinés y los malamutes y los mexicanos sin pelos.**

24

Big dogs and small dogs and short dogs and tall dogs.
Perros grandes y perros pequeños y los perros bajitos y los perros altos.

The End.

El fin

## About the dogs in this book.

**1. Beagle-** One of a breed of small hounds having short legs, drooping ears and a smooth coat with white, black, and tan markings.

**Beagle-** Uno de la raza hound pequeño que tiene patas cortas, las orejas sueltas, la piel suave, un abrigo blanco y negro, con manchas cremas.

**2. Bulldog –** A short-haired dog of a breed characterized by a large head, strong square jaws with dewlaps, and a stocky body.

**Bulldog-** Una raza de pelo orto con cabeza grande, tiene la quijada fuerte con papadas, y un cuerpo stocky.

**3. Chihuahua -** A very small dog of a breed originating in Mexico, having pointed ears and a smooth coat.

**Chihuchua-** Un perro muy pequeño de raza que se originó en México, con orejas de puntas y la piel suave.

**4. Collies –** A large dog of a breed originating in Scotland as a sheep dog, having long hair and a long, narrow muzzle.

**Collies –** Una raza de perro grande que se originó en escocia para velar a las ovejas, tiene pelo largo y un bozal estrecho.

**5. Dachshund –** A small dog of a breed developed in Germany for hunting badgers, with a long body, a usually short-haired brown or black and brown coat, drooping ears, and very short legs.

**Dachshund –** Una raza de perro pequeño que se desarrolló en Alemania para cazar los tejones, de cuerpo largo, una piel que casi siempre lleva el pelo corto de color marrón, o marrón con negro, las orejas inclinadas, y las patas muy cortas.

**6. Dalmatian –** A dog of a breed believed to have originated in Dalmatia, having a short, smooth white coat covered with black or dark-brown spots.

**Dalmata –** Una raza de perro que se cree que originó en Dalmatia, con la piel corta y suave, blanca y cubierta de manchas negras o marrones oscuras.

7. **Greyhound** – A large slender dog of an ancient breed, having a smooth coat, a narrow head, and long legs, and capable of running swiftly.

   **Galgo** – Un perro grande y delgado de una raza antigua, que tiene la piel suave, la cabeza estrecha, patas largas, y es capaz de correr rápidamente.

8. **Husky** – A dog of a breed developed in Siberia for pulling sleds, having a dense, furry, variously colored coat. 2. A dog similar to a husky of a breed of Arctic origin.

   **Husky** – Una raza de perro desarrollada en la Siberia para llevar a los trineos, con piel densa peludo, de varios colores. 2. Un perro similar al husky de la raza del origen ártico.

9. **Malamutes** – Any of a powerful breed of dogs developed in Alaska as a sled dog, having a thick grey, black, or white coat.

   **Malamutes** – Uno de las razas de perros fuertes que se desarrollarón en Alaska como perro de trineo, que tiene la piel gris, negra o blanca.

10. **Mastiff** – A large dog of an ancient breed, probably originating in Asia, having a short fawn-colored coat.

    **Mastiff** – Una raza antigua de perro grande, que probablemente se originó en Asia, que tiene la piel corta del color del ciervo.

11. **Mexican hairless** – A small dog of a breed of unknown origin, found in Mexico, having a smooth hairless body except for tufts on the head and tail

    **Perro Mexicano sin pelos** – Una raza de perro pequeño de origin desconocido, que se encuentra en México, y tiene el cuerpo suave sin pelo con la excepción de penachos en la cabeza y en la cola.

12. **Miniature** – Something small of its class.

    **Miniatura** – Algo pequeño de su clase

**13. Pekingese** – A toy dog of a breed developed in China, having a flat nose, a long-haired coat, and short, bowed forelegs.

**Pekines** – Una raza de perro pequeño que se desarrolló en la China, que tiene una nariz plana.

**14. Poodle** – Any of a breed of dogs originally developed in Europe as hunting dogs, having thick, curly hair, and ranging widely in size.

**Puli** – Cualquier raza de perro que se desarrolló originalmente en Europa como perro de caza, que tiene el pelo grueso, rizado y de varios tamaños.

**15. Rottweiler** – A German breed of dog having a stocky body, short black fur, and tan face markings.

**Rottweiler** – Una raza de perro Aleman que tiene el cuerpo stocky, pelo negro corto, con manchas cremas en la cara.

**16. Saint Bernard** – A large strong dog of a breed developed in Switzerland, having a thick brown and white coat, originally used by monks of the hospice of Saint Bernard in the Swiss Alps to help patrol the snow-covered region.

**San Bernardo** – Un perro grande y fuerte de una raza que se desarrolló en Suiza, que tiene una piel gruesa del color marrón o blanca, que originalmente fue usada por los monjes del hospice de San Bernardo en las moñatanas de Suiza

**17. Terrier** – Any of various usually small, active dogs originally bred for hunting animals that live in burrows.

**Terrier** – Cualquier perro entre varios que usualmente son pequeños y activos, que se criarón originalmente para la caza de animals que viven bajo la tierra.

**18. Welsh Corgi** – A dog of a breed originating in Wales, having a long body, short legs, and a foxlike head.

**Corgis Galés** – Una raza de perro que se originó en el país de Gales, que tiene el cuerpo largo, las patas cortas y la cabeza como el zorro.

## About the Author

Ann Miller is a mother and grandmother. She published her first book entitled "I Love Birds," in August of 2004. It received wide acceptance, and, it is a favorite of preschoolers and the early elementary age group. I Love Birds is also a favorite of early learning science teachers.

Proverbs, Prayers and Poems for Children and Teens published in April of 2006 is Ann's first inspirational work. This book is a favorite of parents and Sunday school teachers. The prayers and poems in this book inspire and comfort adults and children of all ages.

I Love Dogs is the second book in Ann's I Love Animals series. It is sure to be a favorite of all dog lovers. Ann has included Spanish and English for her bilingual fans. Ann's goal is to strengthen the skills of the beginning reader and to make reading fun. The last two books in the four book series: I love Cats, and I Love Horses will follow soon.

Ann has a bachelor's degree in Business Administration and a Masters in Social Science. She resides in Queens, New York.

Ann's books can be purchased on line at jaylilpublishing.com, other major on line stores, as well as some local bookstores. If you cannot find it in your neighborhood, ask your bookseller to order it.

For more information contact:
Jaylil Publishing Company
Post Office Box 656551 Flushing, New York 11365
Phone: 718 279 2867
Cell: 404 550 1854
Email: jaylilpublishing@aol.com
Web site: jaylilpublishing.com